# Shattering Air

Poems by
**David Biespiel**

**Foreword by Stanley Plumly**

BOA Editions, Ltd. ❧ Brockport, NY ❧ 1996

LC #: 95–83234
ISBN: 1–880238–34–9 cloth
ISBN: 1–880238–35–7 paper

First Edition
96 97 98 99   7 6 5 4 3 2 1

Publications by BOA Editions, Ltd.—
a not-for-profit corporation under section 501 (c) (3)
of the United States Internal Revenue Code—
are made possible with the assistance of grants from
the Literature Program of the New York State Council on the Arts,
the Literature Program of the National Endowment for the Arts,
the Lannan Foundation,
as well as from the Rochester Area Foundation Community Arts Fund
administered by the Arts & Cultural Council for Greater Rochester,
the County of Monroe, NY,
and from many individual supporters.

Cover Design: Geri McCormick
Cover Art: *Ocean Park No. 66*, 1973, by Richard Diebenkorn,
Courtesy of Albright-Knox Art Gallery, Buffalo, New York,
Gift of Seymour H. Knox, 1974.
Author Photo: Alan J. deLay
Typesetting: Richard Foerster
Manufacturing: McNaughton & Gunn, Lithographers
BOA Logo: Mirko

BOA Editions, Ltd.
A. Poulin, Jr., President
92 Park Avenue
Brockport, NY 14420

*for Tricia*

# CONTENTS

## Part Three

# FOREWORD

I t is a test of the seamlessness of his art that David Biespiel so constantly finds the "ruminant undercurrent" of his subjects without ever sacrificing their actuality. And it is all the more remarkable in a first book that this undercurrent—what Wordsworth once call "the imminent soul in things"—should so effectively supersede appearances. If this sounds a grand pre-scription, in Biespiel's hands it is not. He finds his vitality and subtlety in the commonplace as well as the luminous moment, in contemplation as much as verbal action. Indeed, for Biespiel, stillness is an act, thinking a way of allowing the subject to move into the light, and become the light, as if the inwardness of an experience were its substance.

> As if to draw the light to the body.
> As if to draw the light.
> As if through the hand that is music, that is stillness.
> The bedrock we sat on thrummed like the light.
> Air knew of long presences breaking near the heart.

This is the beginning stanza of *Shattering Air,* and it starts a sequence of poems in which "long presences" dominate, "one body passing through another." Light is its natural, and spiritual, metaphor, and offers Biespiel both the silence and the fluidity he needs. Light also permits him to move within the universal scale. On one hand it can be the sun that "burns the mist with its one blink" or "a river's needle." On the other hand it can be nothing more than "a brightening of the nuthatch's / Plump red breast, one tree to the next" or "dusk-colors . . . out of the air."

Biespiel makes no claims that his sense of the light, whether indwelling or reflective, is necessarily numinous. It is, instead, the norm of his vision, the level of his insight: it is his way of seeing the world both regaled and revealed, taken for what it is as a source of wonder.

> The rain slants toward the willow.
> The live oak lords over its drizzly solitude,

Sure of its long life. The moon is out there.
The sun stands-to. Air frets.
There's a ripeness here, loud as the one crow
Chewing up sunlight, working
Its kingdom-come on the roof's edge. . . .

Here he is able to bring the source of light down to earth and give it new, palpable, friendly life in the bark of the crow—a sound, as he names it late in the poem, "of dust in the mouth." And while elsewhere the ripeness and glistening may be God-heavy "dew on our heads," it is also only the "strange joy crystallized/ In the dew on a dandelion petal. . . ."

There is, of course, "the yellow light of sorrow too." Perhaps the strongest undercurrent throughout *Shattering Air* is the grieving—this slanting of the light—that seems to dramatize, even at times allegorize, the pensive, contemplative moment. Biespiel is essentially a poet of the natural world, and when it comes to nature, grief is invariably in the eye and heart of the beholder. It should be no surprise that Biespiel's sense of presences is shaded by a melancholy that in another century would be labeled Romantic, but Romantic in expansive, embracing terms, the way Wordsworth can turn the least domestic or wistful experience into something permanently stained with truth. Biespiel may see where "the great clouds span like phantoms / Bearing blood, water, flower, sky. . ." but he is nevertheless aware that in any give instance "All that we know / Constructs a life at this moment." In American, I suppose Biespiel writes like an old-fashioned Transcendentalist, "My mind like rain," seeing worlds within worlds. Yet his wonderful insight and melancholy resonate beyond mere transformation.

If light is the principal nomenclature of his book, then love—passional as well as redemptive—is its prevalent theme. It is the lambent value placed on the meaning of its whole perception. It is the basis for revelation in the presence of the lover ("There Were No Deer in the Thicket," "Each Touch the Future") and for identification with an animate, separate yet sympathetic nature ("Toward Metaphor," "Lilacs"). And it is the consciousness that sustains longer, more narrative, meditative broods on memory and its losses ("Holy Water," "What Gifts of

Love or Quiet Joy"). Biespiel's emotional gift is inclusive, his artistic gift selective. Which is why his poems feel full and airy at the same time. Love is an attitude as much as it is the issue—and love, for Biespiel, is the lightness of being itself. In one place, a poem entitled "A Love Story" begins with a beautiful distraction: "The snows fell in the hundred acres behind the farmhouse." In another place, in a poem entitled "To a Sanderling," the object is evoked with touches:

> The light atones for small things:
> Fire, songs, quiet particles of breath
>
> Blown out through your potato-white belly,
> Through your thin cigar beak, legs
> Dididilying back
> And forth with the tide, dim mist like needle
> Points, tender even, and dull.

The atoning light—that is the image and reality Biespiel's poems abide in, as if the poetry of a thing will save its soul. His poetic forms are understated, like the light within and around them, and build from richly qualified particulars, as though their occurrence were spontaneous and ruminative with the thought at the moment. When in fact his poems are achievements. Some of his lines speak with the brevity of the note-taker; some lines extend with the gratitude of the worshipper. Still others—and these are the majority—fill to running over the pentameter. "Dancing Children":

> Like the veins in a finger waves clip onto the sandbars.
> Surfers coast out and rise. Crests rise with them. Then fall
> Without a moan. They dig into the shore, recede, push out.
> Dune grass with its dark hair fills onlookers with hope.
> One puts a hand to her cheek. One, like a shell, to her ear.
> One waves and waves to the falling circle of small children.
> They sing in the tidepools. Their old bridges fall.

This poem only gets better, and bigger. What one senses in these lines is the pressure rather than the weaning presence of the speaker—a speaker willing to stand apart from the clarity and humanity of the event while able to be at the same time its passionate witness. How little does Biespiel enter his poems. How little does he need to.

—Stanley Plumly

*Part One*

# THERE WERE NO DEER IN THE THICKET

As if to draw the light to the body.
As if to draw the light.
As if through the hand that is music, that is stillness.
The bedrock we sat on thrummed like the light.
Air knew of long presences breaking near the heart.

Yesterday is already given up,
Like a body passing through another,
The voices dissolving the way light falls on the hand,
The way humility is given up.
You said the poplars made a music like daylight—

What the black spot in the eye catches—
Strumming the afternoon fissure to an answer.
You said the grass was not familiar,
That the ruminant undercurrent slapped at the green blades.
The wind was not an answer, not a music.

You said: *Look, deer!*
You said: *Give me your hand again.*
What of the light, full of voices, blowing streaks
Through the vigil-less holes in every moment?
*Give me your hand again.*

You slept, light softest on your closed eyelids.
Your breath.
Gray dimming in the bedrock.
There were no deer in the thicket, teething the grass,
Lying in the lion's sun.

Always someone is missing whom I'll never meet, never touch.
Even the poplars are full of grief.
You said the light was like Canada, vast.
You said the heart will break for anyone,
Never more than a body from another.

# IN THE DREAM I'M RUNNING

Out the back door. Over a bleak
Rise to the ocean. The beach lifts
Out of the dawn-mist grace of the air.
Out of the faint dunes' fenceless sheen.
The sun burns the mist with its one blink.
It shines on the sandshale, on the seasalt,
And the white-skinned waves. The water
Another journey worth floating out into.

The tide breaking, easing back.
The child I wouldn't keep
Whispers in the tern's flight,
Falls in my arms. Turns, falls.
Eyes gone blank. Forgetting the world
Never seen. The child blowing
Its only breath into the other life.

# THAT VOICE, THOSE PETALS

Black and white butterflies. Purple
Buds on the crumbweed. Up
Through the miner's lettuce.
In coffee cans: pansies, begonias.
I think of reefer and Sam Adams' face—
Brewer, patriot, rising hairline.
The gold-tubed wind chime keeps on.
19 bucks at the K-Mart. Looked refined
Before the rust. Keeps on
Like a longshoreman's heart, Fridays,
When he cops a pint and a loaf of bread.
Summer light hard on his eyes: driving west.
The Ford running good for a change.
Reek of salt on his hands, O.K. with solitude.
He sees something red growing like a dress
In the medians he can't identify.
Mother can, has told him. Time
And again. That voice.
*Why can't you listen? You don't listen.*

# AT TWENTY-EIGHT THOUSAND FEET

What you can't see of the earth's cut and paste—
A river's needle, lines of trees greening,
Roadway lanes in composition without motive,
All the buses let out by a bell—is nothing
Compared to these white islands of clouds
Burning to distraction. Both are anonymous.
If you could see to whatever point in the sky
You wanted to name—as if you could be there
Waiting, anything you thought you were,
That is a thing, like a meditation,
A child would see as a lap, climb there,
And lay the head to rest.
The word that comes to mind: *volcanic.*
The word you speak is something different,
A spray of breath vanishing in the sky's blue streaks:
*Infinitesimal.* Those explosions
Are an earlier mist, sparks the color of ash,
Nothing you could touch, the airplane
Descending like a submarine. What sleep you feel,
Laying the head back, what shapes you fall into,
Whitecap or mountain, resemble swimming in a bay
At morning, mist rimming the beach
And horizon, and hung overhead like a hood
For the body of water—waves inverted,
Easy to swallow—and the blue in the sky brushstroke
When you swim to the buoys, float,
Measure your body halfway under, halfway above,
Trusting the cloud-steam will flame out
By noon, piece by piece, in the actual sky.

# TOWARD METAPHOR

If I were sure this is the place
I'd say so to the long-pointed
Elliptical leaf of the sweet birch,
Say: This is the place, the all-
Blessed in a palm of shadow, all
Of another length of the year gone,
The snow trembling in the breath
I make behind the eyes. I blow.

Here's a white thing. I call it nothing.
Here's a brightening of the nuthatch's
Plump red breast, one tree to the next,
The flight rough, the pale throat.
If I were sure, and if the leaf were
Visible, I'd say *This is the place.*
I'd see what I've brought back,
The singing of the nuthatch so sweet.

And if it's not the one visible,
But my brother calling, his gasp
The open trembling the wind finds
In its loyalty to wandering,
I'd hear his voice's procession
Finding a home, a landscape—
How it falls like the dusk-colors
A life gleams, grinning, out of the air.

Every grief is a night music.
Every song even I can sing
In tune, one key to the next.
It's not this note bringing a brother
Back to the branches
Of the black oak, calling him
Out of the wind. It glittered
When he fell. It hummed.

Now he calls me, his voice a wide
Light turning off, a parable
Of night-fading, the sun up, days
Unfastened. Now he's standing
Behind my eyes and will not give
His hand, will not turn, nor wait,
Nor look when the air is a voice,
When the air is a worshipping hour.

# WHITE ROSES

Men truck I–45 up and down Oklahoma,
Love the railroad, women, and wave ballcaps
To the sunburnt trains. Prairie
Spreads toward mute corn,
Sunflowers, pigsties.
In front lots, bus parts
Scatter like bred dogs.

Out of the caboose one man
Is like a menagerie. Trains chugging
Past towns with decent names,
Sunday to Friday. Whistleblast:
A reminder of old wins
Or terror a veteran
Won't even tell his new wife.
She knows something's happening
Already to their marriage.

His people adore her Chickasaw hair.
She loves the doctor's white roses
And the wood bird,
With the plastic spinning wings,
Poking out of the planters. The withered
Petals, she calls, *etudes*.

❧

# WALKING WITH VIRGIL

Joints in rigor mortis, lips sliced back,
Teeth like hardened salt, toes spread, stiff fur
Cloaked with an oily gray and flat,
The eyes wide-open as it dropped
From his long, dog mouth at my Wellingtons:
This mouse in limbo long before Virgil
Found it in the ivy patch on the path
Below the woods. It was death he smelled,
Its circle of thin-boned living long gone,
And the day nearly lost over the brink.
Virgil looked up and wagged: a gift.
Food for the cave, the pack.
From the dirt the mouse kept staring at us.
Virgil looked down, looked back, then snatched it
Again and trotted down to the brook
Where dusk was soaking in shadelessly
And dropped it in the water. It sank.
Small, circular ripples rose in its place.
As if to keep it in mind forever,
Virgil stared, retriever's head tilted, tail
Still. Light flecked back behind the trees.
Darkness coming on with its heavy arc.
When he came back to me, came back
From that other world, it was as if to say
His stray days were over. Then up the path,
Wagging his tail at half-mast and trotting.
And I, so as not to go astray, following.

# NOTHING BUT LIGHT ON THE MIND

And rain drumming the current
Of its strung-out song, without clarity or desire,
Without the quiet loss this morning
After your body's given back to itself,
Back to the unrehearsed earth
No one gets familiar with.
The rain slants toward the willow.
The live oak lords over its drizzly solitude,

Sure of its long life. The moon is out there.
The sun stands-to. Air frets.
There's a ripeness here, loud as the one crow
Chewing up sunlight, working
Its kingdom-come on the roof's edge,
Mouthing anything but the dead's forgiveness,
That sound of dust in the mouth.

# COUNTRY WESTERN

And last month's bluebonnet slanting over the meadowgrass path no one knows who cut. You could run down the hill fast, almost stumbling, Braes Bayou running sunward, out of sight, and toward the bend that drops into Buffalo Bayou, miles from Galveston Bay, miles from where the gulls, you think, day-trip in autumn: past the gray-wrought, long breakers at San Louis Pass and Madagorda, past the first light warning from the lighthouse at Griffin's Point, past Rio Hondo, past Boca Chica, where they turn above the telephone poles and span their wings and aim their white landing for the dumpsters, almost empty but caked with lice, you figure, and a pom-pom stolen from Friday's McAllen-Edinburg game—that afterward one father swings a blade at another that hardly shines under the halogen lamplight refracting across the dumptruck gravel parking lot, and no one thinks anything of it, as no one thinks anything of the pom-pom stolen from a pickup someone named Lloyd drove someone named Carolyn in and parked at the Stop N Go and went in to buy six-pack cans of Lone Star. But to leap the matter of the bayou, six-feet, you had to climb up again, look over the highway traffic, then run down, take the last footstep half over the water's edge. If someone were watching, you had to learn, right then, to fly. Mind the gull's black-masked flight, and you find yourself on a wire, head to the left, the right, monocular, cloud cover. As in your mind a girl's hand in yours after she's watched you leap. That's why you begin to sing what you heard on the radio, driving to Galveston Island, I-45, hot and long, and a flat haze landing in the afternoon dusk, landing right inside you as a twin-jet touches down alongside at Hobby. You're singing above the reverb: *If Drinking Don't Kill Me (Her Memory Will)*. It's not memory now, but the break and break again of a wave you can't interpret, can't get inside, or love, or take with you when you're gone.

# WHAT GIFTS OF LOVE OR QUIET JOY

The third one. The cold shut out,
Blue tongue and sniffle, first cry,
First blink and breath, quick, unmelodic,
Untied easily, the element of air
Dissembling the light from dark. The pain,
The time that's passed, the time to come,
The unexpected capitulations
The years will settle into, their cold breaths.

Stone-etchings on the heart slab. Rose moss
Sprawls and branches white tufts where the grass stands
And greens, where I stand for the prayer
I memorized, and look over the hedges'
Tongues—five girls at patty-cake, the rise
Of their voices like an urgent fever.
The box beneath me moistens.
I can smell the wood's exquisite fact.

Your hand, your breath. We lie down. We join,
Enter, and rise. We forget the sunlight's
Vernal nerves that petition the air.
You drift asleep. Your throat's wind and bone-white breath
Slumps onto my neck and settles there
Warm as the fever of the unsealed cry,
The halting, the gasps and scratches the half-sense
Alters in the body's core recoiling.

Black-laced, flat-soled leather, untied
Under the bedding hung over the mattress,
The floor's dank wood oily in the old sunlight,
Your father's London trunk from the war,
His father's writing desk, open and gold-keyed,
I sit here, my left foot lifting the shoe,
The white birch outside scraping the window,
The white birch outside scraping the air.

My hands are soft as leather and cold
On my neck and thighs. My fingers rub down
To the leg's horizon, scratch the tufts
Graying on the knee, gray as the cloud's rift
That drifts lightly as a leaf, and eastward.
I hardly need to understand one thing
About this moment, or know dust from flame, sweat
From something other than fate or desire.

It's no wonder we've named it survival.
See how it moves always beneath the feet?
When I stain the bones, I trigger some forgotten
Gasp or cough—it's not my father's or mother's.
It's not the ancestral flare and pulse
I slap at, or grasp and let slip.
It's not the sunlight I block from the eyes.
It's not the eyes, the iris or pupil.

What if I can't listen, can't see anymore?
What gifts of love or quiet joy will I hear
In the frozen night, or observe by day?
Try to shut out the winter's warm element
Of light, or the level grass crushed like teeth.
The clouds and sky, the tongue and breath:
These aren't infected or essential.
I claim no inch on inch of irrevocable body.

I, too, will come to know worm or flame.
I'll leave no trace but the tongue, sponged
And cleaned, hung on a wall like an old photo
Passed on and framed, mellowing, deceptive,
Like the days of a past winter, the sweet
Yellow clover buried in the light snow.
Cheekbone and skull of clover, jowl and seed-
Scattered, the upland grouse still hungry.

—*after Charles Wright*

# I COUNT A HUNDRED FALLING STARS EACH SUMMER

It was dawn. The shoe string of its light broke,
Stalled, blazed. I could trace its topaz life
As it burned backward in time.
That whorl, that moment after
Falling was lined with desire
And lined with the yellow light of sorrow too.
The awe glazing like a sigh

Almost loud enough to stop the night
From turning over: over the live oak's hallowed
Leaves, over the this-way-that-way stillness
In the willow, over the silence blowing
At the other side of all I can remember,
Golden, newborn in the night, any night
Come down, come down from the Texas sky.

# *Part Two*

# DEAD

---

Fog careful of nothing.
Rock moss, spring nasturtiums, goldfinch: unseeable.

The only color, blurred sky, gray as the river.
Where are we? The great road: underwater.

Where we have travelled, gone.
The sand bank, nights that are growing

Into the current, gone.
The shoals and small pools, gone.

People living off hate, early fishermen,
Unrequited lovers, requited lovers,

All gone, and no poets singing of other arts
Or lost boats.

# I THINK OF YOUR EYES

Flame-blue as chicory.
That season of lost light seeping in.
Wind you called *rapture*. Falling stars—
I wanted to pick them up

From the sunken grass
Like glittering bugs.
We held hands, the human pleasure.
Little oracles, the fingers. We listened

And breathed
In the unexpungable
Sky. The thought of God
Was dew on our heads.

# AUTUMN OF THE BODY

Consider the femur, patella, the upper stress through fibula, tibia, phalanges tongued in the shoe. What we call thigh, knee, splint, shin, and toe, a step that follows a step. Consider the arm—humerus, radius, ulna. Or the deltoid, biceps, triceps, and flexor of the wrist, the arteries and nerves rivering to the fingers. Or the hand, what it holds—a ball or pen, a blade of grass, another hand. Or what it lets go, or what it reaches for. Not like the face or the angle of the mouth in a smile or in grief. Or the brow, temple, or cheekbone. Or those familial strains furrowed up, down, and across, deep or shallow. Or the irises' elegies and joys. —I'm twelve again. I walk him to the toilet, unzip and seat him. The arm seems bloodless, spongy, the bone like ice, the crack to slide, the fear, his falling, my standing. I walk him to the bed, the sheets pulled tight. Don't be afraid. This is the body in motion like the wind that clacks at the back gate. I'd seen them from a distance, a window, the black funnels that touch down, shudder, like the whirlwind's cool anatomy in the eye. Afternoons we walk—his fedora's thin felt pulled to the brow, the brim's curl flapping in the wet air. Blades of blown grass stick to the hand and so much rain the leaves fall early, fill the sky with magnolia, slippery elm, live oak. I could tell you he's someone I didn't know, just old. Or I could say he's my great-grandfather, the one who peddled a rag cart in the easy twenties. Either way I'm only a witness. That Sunday when we walk to the end-of-the-block ballfield and sit in the dugout, rain hail-hard, tornado warnings to the north, three starlings in center blink at something final, a falling, unforgettable as the season, gray or black, an odd gauze of light. What I don't forget are their eyes. Not what they see or how they look at us, but how they stay closed for a long time, metallic-blue, no squeak or bubble or whistle. And this other thing: his eyes too are closed. What's more lonely in a dugout than watching rain? Maybe it's holding a bone of grass in the palm and letting the wind find it so it blows. Maybe it's closing the eyelids so you always feel the green in the hand.

# BEFORE THE FIRST LIGHT

It's another dream with no roads, but plenty
Of footsteps. One dark tree, a willow, the leaves
Still affected by the rainwater's wanting.
My body is shaped like a dog,
Lying beside a river, watching the grass
On the other side move. My body moves
In no particular direction.
I lie on my haunches and look at the tree.
Blind to the movement of clouds.
Deaf to the sounds of crow.
The tree is shaped like a woman who's crying.
Her daughter has been hit by a car.
Her leg is broken, the bone snapped.
She is screaming. She is pointing
At her leg and stretching her head back.
A sudden wind and the tree bends. Branches
Stretch against the air, the returning rain.
It is not a woman, but a tree again.
No footsteps in sight, but plenty of road.

# LATE JUNE

July coming not a moment too late,
Bringing its fine steam like breath's mist
Blossoming on air. Childhood
Is everywhere in my sleep, turning over
To one side, then the other, swaying
On its dreamlife of half-recognitions,
The *rickcrick-rickcrick* sound of the swingset
Out back. The robins early to rise

Beyond that, loosened from the shadows
The sun brings up, loosened from the judgeless
Moan of the sun, a strange joy crystallized
In the dew on a dandelion petal,
Strange thoughts resting from the body's flesh,
From the light's flesh, the way lovers rest
And let the morning bear its light over them.

# LILACS

*Allston, Massachusetts, 1985*

Leeward of the house is nothing but the tip-
Tapered leaves and the sweet blooms' purple
And white pyramidal clusters. In the shade
The petals are dark as plums or thumb-sized
Knots of blackberries, though in the sun
They're gray as sea water almost rippling.
When she comes to pick them after school's out,
They lean, as if to weep, into her palms, a few
Sprigs falling to the concrete, the flesh of each

Touching as companions touch. She must know
They'll die, though it's summer she feels
In the smooth oval green when she cracks the stems.
Above her hair that falls straight and black,
Above the wide petals of the early evening
Primrose, right and left of the lilac bushes,
There are only waves of clouds that crumble,
Bulge, and subside. I don't think she cares
About the clouds. They bloom and fall.

She's found a heaven to put in the window.
And I know she doesn't think of my father
At the salvage tug's anchor cable,
Near the Korea Strait's eastern channel.
It's 1951, the sky filled with a close knowledge
Of the gunfire's blue-red clusters of smoke.
He's at the winch, watching the hawser slacken
As it hooks in the damaged vessel.
Punctures the size of plums or blackberries.

Two men, to the right and the left
Of my father, will be shot. They will die.
*Cut down,* he'll say. Unlike the primrose

On each side of the lilacs. So dark,
The top ones beyond any reach or pull
But the wind's, and visible in the lamplight
Where the great clouds span like phantoms
Bearing blood, water, flower, sky.
Those things we never give up.
Be it late spring. Be it cloudy weather.

# IT IS TRUTH AND ITS PARADISE

of warm mouths
I desire of a shoreline, walking, and watching
The thin-legged pipers clip the high tide
And its unflinching breeze. It is the truth
Of the inner voice inside the new
Petals of the rough blazing star
That grows pinkly along the seawall, and nothing
In the first light around it. All that we know
Constructs a life in this moment.

The many voices rise like crystallized secrets
We make with ourselves. The morning comes back.
Temptations in place.
The pure desire is to bend and pick
The blazing star, carry it home to vase
On the windowsill, and to watch the sunlight
Touch the center of its last hour.

# A LOVE STORY

The snows fell in the hundred acres behind the farmhouse.

Crises did not betray us into madness—like looking into a field of pines and seeing elves with knives hidden in their boots.

We sleep in peace.

In rainy weather I praise the clouds for existence, eyes for rejoicing.

Sky is only part of the solution, trembling light only part, wind part: Do leaves fall here as they do in rivers, mile after mile, exquisitely blowing up and down?

Odor of dark eyes retreating from war is where the dream shifted, stone wall, the look of grime and loss, cowless, birdless meadow.

A small girl sits on top, barefoot, twirling a baton like a starfish, crying: Light varies, birds quick, sky the color of char.

On sunny days like today, Sunday, Passion's day, day with no nemesis, all the air is filled with mouths harping at nothing, then a silence like dreaming of the early hours of conception: Water, salt.

Who can know?

You comb your long hair.

To see the small girl's face, with its gold freckles, turn into a cat's paw, to see the cat's paw, white as coral, clawing a trout pushing hard through a river that was the meadow—pushing hard as a conscience.

Love, you do not darken like trees.

# *HIDEAWAY*

I went nowhere to dream as a boy. Clouds kept away. The sun killed me. I kept my fingers in my pockets. Some days I'd tunnel inside bayou pipes on hands and knees. I'd toke butts I'd found in ditches and sing *Dixie* past earshot of my Midwestern mother. A rusted-out harmony. She'd guess it, though. I'd catch a licking. *Crawdad, crawdad, give me your ear, your burly heart.* I've come no better since. I've given up smoke. But kept the light for luck.

# SELF-PORTRAIT AS MANIAC

Stiff elbow, crick-neck,
I awake in the fine state.

Stars wide-eye the yonder,
Fog like sheep's yoke,

Night flushes blood-
Complaints back

Into dew. I don't
Conspire with air

Or wind or sand.
I've stepped aside,

My mind like rain.
God, how will I find the stones

Whittled with sun
And tesseried on the hill

That are motionless as sheep?
They're singing laments.

I must nuzzle with them.

# TOWER

Fifteen years old and naked, quivering,
Stomachs flat on the ten-meter platform
Of a strange pool, 3 o'clock in the morning,
Bonnie Horton and I leaned our heads over
The hard edge of the tower to make out
The liquid surface below us, four arms
Hanging limp, loose, in the 90-degree
Darkness, swaying, knocking each other,
Playfully pulling a wrist hard enough
So one of us would fall into the flat
Blue hole of relief. I kept looking
For the water's wind-ripple, but so dark,
We could barely see the starting blocks
Or the deck chairs. And I could hardly see
The fence we'd snuck over, to climb up, strip
For the first time together, kiss, and touch
Helplessly, hysterically, Bonnie's two
Gold bracelets jingling like laughter,
Not a care but to hold her body
As close to mine as she'd allow,
To reverse-somersault down finally
To cool off. I never wanted to leave
That tower, never wanted to let go
Of a moment that lucky, but suddenly,
In the play and tug, one of her bracelets
Broke—I tried to watch it plummet,
See the splash, jump down to get it.
I couldn't. It bounced. Clink-clink-
Clink on the concrete bottom of the well.
We lay there disordered,
The air rough and shattering, distance
Clenched in our lungs like a giant fist,
The heat lingering. Bonnie said, *O*, or cried,
Softly, I don't remember. Amazed,
I was looking at my hands, and I still wonder

How they could hold pleasure one minute, close
To the lips, touching, wet. Skinless wind
The next. The veins throbbing over the cold depths
As they would the next morning at ten-meter
Workout, at our pool, before my first dive,
A front one-and-one-half with a full twist,
My body tearing the sky, the cool water
Pure, fragrant, taking me whole.

# AGAINST ROMANTICISM

There, in the weeds with yellow daisies, growing by the stone
    fence, in damp sunlight,
Where, sometimes, a barn owl, at dusk, turns its head, no God
    is expected.

Instead, laughing gulls—back from the dump, in small
    groups, like cousins
At their uncle's funeral, who try to mourn, but want to catch
    up, tentatively

Planning for Independence Day, a jaunt, with the kids, to
    Tijuana, all that homegrown
And fried beans, and a languid afternoon walking through
    rug markets, admiring

The hubcaps, figuring the exchange, the prices here with the
    prices at Macy's.
Sometimes, waiting for a clerk, I too secretly fall in love with
    the plastic tulips.

# *Part Three*

# WAITING ROOM

                    The teenage girl
Dropped off by her boyfriend. She's left
To uncoil. Her eyes shut, then open.
You're in the other room, and she's a firefly
Pantomiming the day's conscience. Outside,
Weeks with no rain, no lick of hard air.
Weeks with the sad-faced bulbs
Filling the night's good intentions. After,
We walk the streets under the lush trees.

I throw pebbles at the trunks.
We walk the streets and pause to watch the heat-
Lightning fracture the sky with its white light,
Its firelight, its wide blazing silence
And no name. No one from here to Abilene
Thinks anything of it, though the crickets
Cry and the sky shines.

# RETREAT

Afterglow, or before it, upsets
Like a taut play,
Played daily. Or causes a silence
Like wooddrift in the tide,
And even that troubling
In the tailend, the dire glow
That flattens the ocean
To glass, dull as rust.
Who can remember that
Falling everyday, the pomp
Of the tense sun setting,
And the transfixion, like dream,
Or fear of dream or the dark,
Or dark as dream
Come out of all the universe
In a mind, a moment?
Easier to remember, on a dune,
Standing, a man who watches the day
Die, and for a moment,
Though it is everything but true,
He has hidden from his life.

# HOLY WATER

*for Stanley Plumly*

**1**

Out of the feathery
Ring of the wind chime
That is never silent,
Out of the late autumn evening,
Out of the moon's gray speech:
As if stumbling
Out the swinging door
Of Bud's Catfish
Or Lulu's Chili Shack.
Or the night we drove out
Of Gilley's, 85 miles
Per hour with the headlights off,
George Jones on the radio.
We sang loud as traffic
To *Old Brush Arbors*.
We let our bodies down on the jetty
With the tide high
And the dawnlight
Drifting at our feet,
With the waterline's azure palms
Uncurling and reaching back.
She was a girl I don't remember,
Our feet in the gulfwater,
Whiskey, constellations
Clenching the hour's teeth.

**2**

A silence now
At the end of the telephone wires
Where for twenty-two nights
Chimney swifts gathered

And spun their nuances
In the air's bare longing.
The sun was afraid
To turn the bedding
Of the evenings down.
They wheeled with their tribe
In the shape of a funnel.
Their quick flight
Swam against the currents
Of their palate-black past—
Blown leaves,
Wind from the north.
Like brown sugar
Poured down a bag,
They would pleat back their wings,
Aim their bodies down the alley's chimney,
A hundred, two hundred,
As if diving into water—
Down, down, down,
*Chreeek, chreeek, chreeek,*
They'd cry—
And disappear and cling.
Rising out
Of that infestation sang
A gesture to the trees
To flatter their silhouettes,
The night to ease in,
And the clouds
To say goodbye to nothing,
So that their songs unrolled
Gently on the dreamy occasion
Of the non-occasion.
And morning—oh, the morning
Was a leitmotif for forgetting.


**3**
A life of revelations
Is long as any memory

Cooing in the smooth
Interior of angel wings
Dug out when the tide's out.
I've put them so many
Times to my ear
Just thinking of it
I can curl into the sand
From where they came—
Swimming beneath sea-craters,
Among star-shaped crabs
And lost sails,
Sun singing down
To the darkest caves.
That was beauty, too,
Solitary, good, mired in love.


**4**

Last time I saw that girl
Was a New Year's Eve at Gilley's.
She was two-stepping
To *I'd Waltz Across Texas with You*
With the turquoise-broached, string-
Tied drummer who'd downstaged for caterwauls.
Everyone whooped and yeee-hawed.
The girl twirled in her hooped denim dress.
She shined.
She woke up next morning
In a five-a-night motel in Reynosa
And called a week later from a Taco Bell:
*How the hell did I get there?* she asked.
Sleep after sleep, I said—
The body's innuendo,
Interior driftings
Like the edges of water,
Like the sky,
Like meteors unstrung
And blazing
Into unnameable waters of terror.

Hell, I don't remember
How she got there.
I don't remember how I got here.


**5**
A scream
From under the gulfwater,
A farthering,
A longing in the offing,
Dories panting on their ropes,
Jellyfish undulant,
Painting the seafloor
With their gutsy imprints.
Everywhere the throbbing
Voices of gulls, their white hymns,
Mollusks burrowing,
Biding their time,
Shrimp nestling in the sand-ripples
Carrion-scavenging.
The buoys' bony-clang
So far, so far
From the elegant shiver
A body feels
Before falling in love.


**6**
The cut on my chin was from falling
In the 10,000-car parking lot
Outside of Gilley's. What
The gravel felt like:
A thousand fists.
What the sky looked like:
A cave of disbelief.
That was a landscape
Where stars ricocheted,
And I was like a stroke-ruined man
With no senses in the fingers:

So I can't feel fire
Burning them—
And won't know
Without the smell of the burning skin.


**7**

When elegists cry out
In their chorus
Of a thousand voices,
Every heart is sluggish
And can only calibrate desire
By counting ten underwater.
We're all holy,
We're all scratching poorly
In a rearrangement of afterlives.


**8**

Now the IV come undone—
Now my father's hand—
Now the rubber tube lined with blood—
The line out of here, snow
Nowhere but imagined,
February, bluebonnets,
Blinds half-open.
Looking out the hospital window,
The twelve-year-old boy
Who I was
Could see the souls
Of parking lot lights
Glowing all night.
Beyond that the highway to the gulfwater,
Where, if I could,
I'd be at that moment,
Crouching in the tideline.
I'd cup water
Into my two hands
And cleanse my face:

Now his hand, his breath.
I don't want to go back
To that season where grass stays brown
As if on fire.
I don't want to lift him up again
Onto the gurney.


**9**
There's a sign
I can't forget above Interstate 45
Crossing one night into Oklahoma:
LET'S MAKE OKLAHOMA THE BORN AGAIN STATE.
The night that girl disappeared
Like a small bird
We ate catfish and fried shrimp.
We danced at Gilley's
And rode the mechanical bronco.
Even as this memory rings in my ear
It's conditioned on the waves breaking
In rhythm that night,
The moon broken in half,
Reflecting and fraying
In the troughs and the mild crests.
I could have slept
And never woke,
Throbbing and sighing
On the hammock of the seawall.
I could have dreamed of fire's rapture
Marching touchless roads
Through oak or magnolia.
Pulses of smoke,
That blue thing,
Rising from a chimney.


**10**
Maybe the moon is a drowning child
Rising and falling back.

Maybe the stars are unborn desires.
The forget-me-nots
Droop on the three-legged table
Like jellyfish in low waves.
Sometimes on the beach for hours
With crickets nearby,
Dusk searing the air
To the edge of rain,
I veer into scrubgrass
And gather prairie smoke,
Fruit plumy as a feather duster.
I smell the soft hairs breathing
And save the roots for tea.
What the hands feel is temporal,
Like the nightly moon,
Or the idea of it,
Waving recklessly from beyond the offing,
And nothing in the sunrise
But a bell, repeating its own name,
Somewhere, far off.


## 11

Think of the view from a bridge:
The water's slow current of leaves
And wood-drift, rocks
Half-exposed and moaning
Into themselves.
Think of a barn door left open
Where birds fly through
One end and out the other.
Think of the dream
Of a father spreading kerosene
Over the yard, torching the grass,
Knowing west winds will blow the fire lakeward.
What occasion does wind keep with the house?
What cow will *moo*
Goodnight to the moon?
I say *goodnight, father,*

Standing in the hissing yard.
The moon is not rising.
It's folding to sleep.


**12**
Massive dark, frost. All
I could see from atop the seawall
Was wind and waves.
Where the stranger came from,
Cutting into the tide,
I'll never know.
I wished it was the jetty she'd gone to,
To levy her dreams and throw lilies
At the tide-breaks.
The voice I heard
Through her body—
Part scream, part laughter—
Reminded me of leaves
Disappearing in darkness.
She waded back to shore,
Lifted and opened
The foamy-white
Headstone of her hand,
And waved hello.

# RUTH IN THE FIELDS

*two poems for my mother*

**1**

Wind like a long question among us.
Even the pasture won't answer,
Remembering light that little by little
Evens the dusk, little by little crosses
The slow grass. Stars are migrants
Who pause at the river. They question the sky,
The breezes, like souls. Your mother
Sets down her bags to rest and fears nothing.
Blood still falls through her, still rises.
Touch her hand, stars blaze.
Touch her hand, light marbles.


**2**

Now wind, like a bird in flight, shifts
As if pausing inside a body.
In dreams, she walks among barley
Or wheat, blackbirds everywhere
On the ground, in flight. Or she's in a valley
Of poppies that are like red hands
Of the Lord, waving mildly. Now wind
Lets its wings down, down through her hair.
Now she asks for water, still thirsty
From the last mornings of her life.

# THE HEAT SOURS

And squeezes through the blinds of the open window,
The light foliated, inflamed. The heat turns
To dust over the sliced lemons
And saddens itself. Its breath like a child's
Sleeping breath, sleeping on the grass,
Oak-shadow and windbreak driving away
The gnats coming on with the sun.
With the waxwings: if one let me crawl within the sound

Of its breathing, its brown, warm belly
Rising and falling, would the song in its voice
Settle? And rest? Would it fly to a willow twig
And call out to the wounds of heaven,
Heaven on earth, earth we give our bodies to?
Or I put an ear to the grass, accepting
The urge not to cry again? At anything?

# TO A SANDERLING

The tide like a shelf—what is there but God's
Own idea of belief,
Good friend? Love or knowledge? Valiant winks?
The lute-like steps that you make?
The waves strumming along with night? The fog?

Your prologues: They're receding
Like foam, like the peaceful footsteps washed-up
Sand dollars shadow, evade
In the next curriculum of breaking
Waves. And some deep virtue. Here,

Water glistens as through stained glass, with red rings,
And blue, the shown ablution
Patterned in light and labelled "forgiveness."
The light atones for small things:
Fire, songs, quiet particles of breath

Blown out through your potato-white belly,
Through your thin cigar beak, legs
Dididilying back
And forth with the tide, dim mist like needle
Points, tender even, and dull.

Good friend, your ineffable
Running nearly illuminates watery
Myths, ugly or beautiful, that we cull
From life's fingerprint. You know:
From the clean villages, from bloodletting,

From beating and beating nights of the sea,
Undulant, changeless, moon by
Moon, and faithful as a landlocked prophet.
Sleepless, he thinks of you. The
Lulls, the silent work, the godless faith.

# THE CLOCK IN THE NURSERY

**1**

It sounds like dirt thrown on a casket.
The rain.

The white-washed walls
In this house like smudges.

A child stops in a night hallway, pushes
Through a door's threshold,
Climbs back between his parents bodies,
Somewhere, in this city.

Waking me is heavy wind
Pressing against the windows.

**2**

All day the brows
Of women and children were penitent
With ash.

Like people in a dream
They sacrifice,
Dragging their best hopes through chilly houses.

**3**

In the alleys, in the fig-ruined dunes,
Flashing in the open Pacific,

Will rain leave an imprint,
Like a mind's,
Far enough away from human trills?

**4**

In the dream before waking:

I hear the spirals of robin song.
As if, at this edge of the continent,
Such weeping
Could go on endlessly.


**5**

To straighten my son's 2-year-old legs,
I must needle through one hall
And try not to be afraid of dying.

The faceclock ticks like rain in the wall.
Stuffed bears stare through their hard eyes.

# EACH TOUCH THE FUTURE

To say *yes*, a whisper, *yes*, a nerve.
*Mornings, mornings*: the foghorns' song.
The stiff-backed surf-fishermen cluster,
Undiluted, around the blueing bass. Steam
Rises from its gills that still open.
Gulls hang on in the sky when I enter
You again, as in a dream of flying—
The beginnings of air seen or felt

Or fallen into. As into water.
You are not water but a body
I know, each dune in your wrist.
*Mornings, mornings*: the foghorns unbroken.
Like words, you keep rising under
So that we are, when we are, one air.

# THE DYING COME BACK

Like the only cool moment of summer
In the dry soil, in brown grass.
You have to lie there where wind gets low
The way lovers can who can't stop remembering
To each other. A hand through hair,
A hand pausing at the top of the neck,
Blood coming back. It's only wind carrying
The crow's call, calling and searing the air.

It's only the heartbreak and split-
Fall of a wave, then another,
Unpolished comings and goings.
Meanderless questions the dead
Ask in my sleep: *How many times to swim*
*These waters? How many times on the sand,*
*Under the nameless sun, to lay the body down?*

# DANCING CHILDREN

Like the veins in a finger, waves clip onto the sandbars.
Surfers coast out and rise. Crests rise with them. Then fall
Without a moan. They dig into the shore, recede, push out.
Dune grass with its dark hair fills onlookers with hope.
One puts a hand to her cheek. One, like a shell, to her ear.
One waves and waves to the falling circle of small children.
They sing in the tidepools. Their old bridges fall.

When the children visor their eyes, they watch the steamers
Avoid the rocks. Fog and its wispy lifelines, like centuries,
Behind the wake—centuries with their caverns of joys
Carved with stone and hand on walls that speak, or sing,
Or pass the time from age to age. Voices crying to children
Who know that singing, like crying, is like nothing
If not like the way their hands, in wonder, wrap fingers

Over the ribs of a shell. To feel some legend in the flesh.

# CONSTITUTIONAL

At the top of the grassy dunes. Dogs come to die.
The view is better than the news. Lovers
File out of their sleeping bags. The foghorn sheds its light.
Gulls and pipers queue with both feet. Traffic crawls.
Helicopters clonk back to Oakland, paying me no mind. Me, too.
Call it Zen or not giving a damn. All at once:
A thousand and one eyes are blinking,
And the eucalyptus ring their bark in the air's fervent splinters
That hum or not without toil. So much is said
About *Journeying Toward the Other*. Could be no better
Than a flea biting a dog's paw. Fly on, soldier.

# *ACKNOWLEDGMENTS*

Thanks to the editors who published these poems, some in different versions, in the following magazines:

*Antioch Review*: "Lilacs";
*Denver Quarterly*: "Constitutional";
*G.W. Review*: "Tower";
*The Journal*: "What Gifts of Love or Quiet Joy";
*Ohio Review*: "There Were No Deer in the Thicket";
*The Plum Review*: "Holy Water";
*Poetry Northwest*: "At Twenty-Eight Thousand Feet," "Autumn of
    the Body";
*River City*: "Before the First Light";
*Sou'wester*: "Toward Metaphor";
*ZYZZYVA*: "Hideaway," "Ruth in the Fields."

"In the Dream I'm Running," "Nothing but Light on the Mind," "I
Count a Hundred Falling Stars Each Summer," "Late June," "It Is
Truth and Its Paradise," "Waiting Room," "The Heat Sours," and
"The Dying Come Back" were published as a single sequence, "On
Earth As It Is in Heaven," in *The Journal*.

"Walking with Virgil" appeared in *Dog Music: A Poetry Anthology*,
edited by Joseph Duemer and Jim Simmerman, St. Martin's Press
(New York).

"Lilacs" was reprinted in *The Hermit Kingdom: Poems of the Korean War*,
edited by Paul M. Edwards, Kendall-Hunt Publishing Company
(Dubuque, Iowa).

Thanks also for the support of a Wallace Stegner Fellowship at
Stanford University, the Richard H. Thornton Writer-in-Residence
appointment at Lynchburg College, and an Individual Artist Award
in Poetry from the Maryland Arts Council.

# ABOUT THE AUTHOR

David Biespiel was born in Oklahoma in 1964 and grew up in Texas. He has degrees from Boston University and University of Maryland. A contributor to *American Poetry Review, Antioch Review, The New York Times Book Review,* and *Poetry Northwest,* he is a recipient of the Academy of American Poets Award, the Individual Artist Award in Poetry from the Maryland Arts Council, and a Wallace Stegner Fellowship. He has taught at several universities, most recently at Stanford University. He currently lives in Portland, Oregon.

# BOA EDITIONS, LTD.

## NEW POETS OF AMERICA SERIES

Vol. 1    *Cedarhome*
          Poems by Barton Sutter
          Foreword by W.D. Snodgrass

Vol. 2    *Beast Is a Wolf with Brown Fire*
          Poems by Barry Wallenstein
          Foreword by M.L. Rosenthal

Vol. 3    *Along the Dark Shore*
          Poems by Edward Byrne
          Foreword by John Ashbery

Vol. 4    *Anchor Dragging*
          Poems by Anthony Piccione
          Foreword by Archibald MacLeish

Vol. 5    *Eggs in the Lake*
          Poems by Daniela Gioseffi
          Foreword by John Logan

Vol. 6    *Moving the House*
          Poems by Ingrid Wendt
          Foreword by William Stafford

Vol. 7    *Whomp and Moonshiver*
          Poems by Thomas Whitbread
          Foreword by Richard Wilbur

Vol. 8    *Where We Live*
          Poems by Peter Makuck
          Foreword by Louis Simpson

Vol. 9    *Rose*
          Poems by Li-Young Lee
          Foreword by Gerald Stern

Vol. 10   *Genesis*
          Poems by Emanuel di Pasquale
          Foreword by X.J. Kennedy

Vol. 11   *Borders*
          Poems by Mary Crow
          Foreword by David Ignatow

Vol. 12   *Awake*
          Poems by Dorianne Laux
          Foreword by Philip Levine

Vol. 13   *Hurricane Walk*
          Poems by Diann Blakely Shoaf
          Foreword by William Matthews